The Picnic

by Bobby Lynn Maslen
pictures by John R. Maslen

Scholastic Inc.

New York • Toronto • London • Auckland • Sydney • Mexico City • New Delhi • Hong Kong

Available Bob Books®:

<u>Level A</u>:   Set 1 - First!   Set 2 - Fun!

<u>Level B</u>:   Set 1 - Kids!   Set 2 - Pals!

<u>Level C</u>:   Set 1 - Wow!

Ask for Bob Books at your local bookstore, visit www.bobbooks.com, or call: 1-800-733-5572.

ISBN 0-439-17587-9

12 11 10 9 8 7 6   2 3 4 5/0
Printed in the U.S.A.   10

Jill likes Tim. She likes the beach. Jill had a good idea. Jill fixed a big picnic.

She had hotdogs and buns.
She had green peas and beans.

She had meatballs and
peanut butter. She had
peaches and cream.

Jill made hot tea. She put the
hot tea into a teapot.

She put the picnic in a basket.
It was a feast!

Jill put the picnic and the teapot
into a big box. She went to the
beach. She saw Tim sitting in the sand.

Tim sat by the sea. The sun
was hot. The sand was warm.

Jill and Tim went for a swim. It was a treat to swim in the chilly sea.

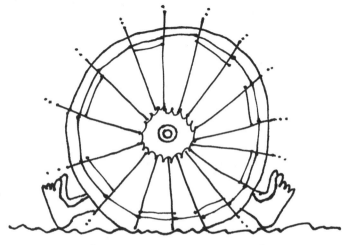

Then they sat on the beach
under a big umbrella. It was
time to eat the picnic.

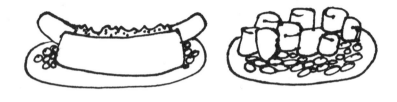

Jill ate a hotdog and bun.
Tim ate meatballs. Jill ate
peas. Tim ate beans.

Tim and Jill had peaches and cream. They sipped tea as they sat by the sea.

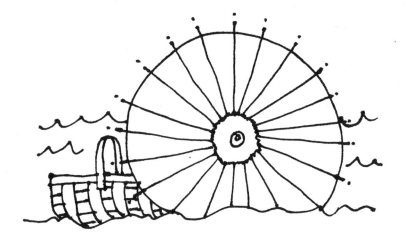

It was good to sit in the sun. It was fun to swim in the sea. It was a treat to eat a picnic at the beach.

The End

Book 4 adds:

Long Vowel Combination:
ea   -   peas